# TWICE TOLD TALES

Twicetold Tales is published by Stone Arch Books
A Capstone Imprint
1710 Roe Crest Drive
North Mankato, Minnesota 56003
www.capstonepub.com

Library of Congress Cataloging-in-Publication Data
            Snowe, Olivia.
  Cassie and the Woolf / by Olivia Snowe; illustrated by
Michelle Lamoreaux.
      p. cm. -- (Twicetold tales)
  Summary: Caleb Woolf has designs on the basket of
food that Cassie Cloak takes to her grandmother every
Sunday, so they set a trap to teach him a lesson.
  ISBN 978-1-4342-3786-6 (library binding) -- ISBN
978-1-4342-6278-3 (paper over board)
1. Fairy tales. 2. Folklore--Germany. [1. Fairy tales.
2. Folklore.]  I. Lamoreaux, Michelle, ill. II. Little Red
Riding Hood. English. III. Title.
  PZ7.S41763Cas 2013
  398.20943--dc23
                            2013002779

Designer: Kay Fraser
Vector Images: Shutterstock

Printed in the United States of America in
Stevens Point, Wisconsin.
032013      007227WZF13

# Cassie
## and the Woolf

by Olivia Snowe

illustrated by Michelle Lamoreaux

▼▼ STONE ARCH BOOKS™

You know the story.

You've heard it before.

Everyone has.

Now, read it again.

A new twist. A new gasp.

The story is told again.

TWICETOLD.

# 1

Cassie Cloak held her red raincoat closed at the neck. Thunder clapped and the rain fell hard in big, swollen drops. The corners and curbs vanished under deepening puddles as piles of snow—still sitting where they'd been pushed aside during winter—melted, joining the torrents of rain.

Before long, downtown Forestville was half flooded.

Cassie jumped from bit of sidewalk to bit of curb, avoiding the deeper puddles. Still, the water sloshed up and into her rubber boots, soaking her favorite rainbow socks. By the time she reached Maurice's Deli, she could hardly keep her footing.

The bell dinged as she pushed through the heavy glass door. She shook off as best she could and dragged her feet along the long black mat toward the counter.

Maurice himself stood behind the high counter, his hands folded on the glass, with his red and white paper hat just a little crooked on his bald head.

"Hello, little Cassie," he said. He always called her that: "little Cassie."

Cassie used to like that nickname. She wasn't little anymore, though. She'd turn thirteen next month. She was out here—in the rain, right in downtown Forestville—all by herself.

Do little kids turn thirteen and go downtown all by themselves? No.

"Hi," Cassie said. "Um, I'm picking up the order for my grandma."

Maurice frowned at the girl and shook his head. "Yes, little Cassie," he said. "I know this. You've been in here to pick up your grandma's Sunday dinner order for as long as I can remember."

Even when she'd make the trip with her mom, Cassie had always been there to pick up the meal.

The meal was always the same. It came in a box, holding two plastic shopping bags. In each plastic bag, there'd be two paper bags. And the paper bags would be filled to bursting with soups and noodle casseroles and sandwiches and pickles.

Every once in a while, Grandma would add some treat to the order: a couple of slices of honey cake or a big square of halvah.

"It's heavy today," Maurice said with a wink. He came around the counter in that uneven shuffle he had, like one of his knees refused to bend.

"It smells delicious," Cassie told him. "I can't wait."

With both arms, Cassie took the cardboard box. The wonderful smells wafted up into her face and the steam fogged her glasses. "Thanks," she said.

"I'll get the door for you," Maurice said. He shuffled past her and she heard the ding-a-ling of the bell over the door.

She thanked him again and stepped back out into the rain.

Once outside, she had to adjust her bags. Maurice had tied the plastic grocery bags tight, but Cassie didn't think they'd hold for long. The cardboard box would probably disintegrate before she made it three blocks to her grandma's apartment building.

Instead of walking on, she hurried under the awning of the office next door. There, she leaned against the big plate window to wait for the rain to slow down, even a little bit.

# 2

Caleb Woolf didn't care. The rain poured over him in sheets. It collected in his matted hair—too long and ragged, like it had been shorn with a pair of a lawn shears—and ran down the back of his neck and the bridge of his nose.

He grinned. He always grinned. His teeth were too big and too white, and even most of his friends thought he might lunge for them and take a bite.

With his back to the basket, Caleb dribbled the ball in front of him, using his legs and back as a shield, protecting it from his defender. It was a game of two-on-two half-court basketball.

"Hit me!" called out Caleb's teammate, Finn Transom.

But Caleb wouldn't pass. The score was ten up, and the next two-point basket would win the game. He wasn't about to hand off that glory to anyone. He'd get those two points himself.

"Come on, Woolf," said Andrew Hunter, the defender. Caleb could feel Andrew's big hand on his back. "Make a move."

Caleb's smile widened. He jerked his head one way, then stepped the other. He dribbled far out in front of him, where Andrew had no chance to steal. Then Caleb pulled up, stopping suddenly. Andrew slipped on the wet cement, and Caleb lifted the basketball and shot.

Two points. Caleb clapped once. "Nice try, boys," he said, grinning at Andrew and Andrew's teammate, Otto Blank.

Caleb's teammate—who'd scored a couple of baskets himself—rolled his eyes and checked his phone for the time. "I better get home," he said. "I'm late for supper."

"Yeah, me too," said Andrew. "Not to mention I'm soaked to the bone. My mom's going to skin me alive for staying out in this hurricane."

Caleb cackled. "Hurricane?" he said. "It's a spring shower."

He turned to Otto. "How about you, Otto?" he said. He fired the basketball at him. Otto caught it before it collided with his face—but only just. "Quick game of one-on-one?" Caleb asked. "Come on. I'll give you a five-point lead to start."

"Can't," Otto said. "Homework. Supper." He tossed the ball back to Caleb, who caught it, dribbled it twice, and shot a perfect three-pointer.

"Swish!" he said.

The other three boys gathered their bags and jackets and headed off.

"Honestly," Caleb called after them through the driving rain. "I've never met three bigger babies and mama's boys."

He watched them, calling out insults and taunts, until they turned the corner and disappeared into downtown. He was alone in Forestville Park now, the only one brave or foolish enough to stand in the downpour.

Caleb sat on the metal bench on the edge of the basketball court and took a long swig from his bottle of water. Soon it was empty and his stomach roared.

"Man, I'm hungry," he said. He could have gone home for supper, but with his older brother home from college and his mom's boyfriend over . . .

"I'd rather sit in the rain and starve," he muttered to himself. Then he happened to look up. He happened to glance toward the corner of Fifth Avenue and Eighth Street as a bolt of lightning struck the metal rod at the top of Forestville Tower, blanketing all of downtown with an eerie, pale-blue light, just for that instant.

He happened to spot Cassie Cloak, huddled out of sight under an awning, and clutching a big, heavy-looking box.

A heavy-looking box of food.

# ~3~

Cassie hadn't been standing under the awning long. Or she didn't think she had, anyway. But her mind liked to wander.

She'd been staring out into the rain, letting the sound of the heavy drops and the thunder wash over her. She let it take her mind into the fairy tales of her childhood. She remembered Mr. Jenkins's kindergarten class.

It was a rainy afternoon like this one—when it got as dark at one in the afternoon as it ought to get at one in the morning. Mr. Jenkins turned off all but one light in the classroom, and Cassie and the rest of the class sat cross-legged around his chair, eager for a story.

He told them about the Frog Prince, and about Snow White and her dwarfs, and about Red Riding Hood. She'd been Cassie's favorite, of course, because Cassie's raincoat was red.

She always bought red raincoats, ever since then.

Before long it must have been six. The sound of Maurice's shop door slamming shook her from her daydreaming.

"I'm closing up, little Cassie," said the old deli man. "Hadn't you better hurry along? You shouldn't dally around downtown when all the shops are closed. It's not safe."

"I will, Maurice," Cassie replied. She peeked out from under the awning, up at the dark and heavy sky. "Just waiting for this rain to let up a little."

Maurice jogged through the rain, holding his jacket over his head. When he got to Cassie, he stooped and smiled at her, and he wiped the rain from his face. "I can give you a ride," he said. "Grandma's over at the Tall Pines Apartments, right?"

Cassie nodded. "Yes," she said. "But I'm fine. I'm sure this won't last."

Maurice frowned at her. "Are you sure?" he said. "It's no bother."

Under the dim street lamps, with the rainwater still on his beaklike nose and dripping from his big hairy ears, Maurice didn't look like himself. In some ways he did—he was obviously Maurice—but it was like Cassie was seeing him for the first time.

She took a step back and tried to smile. "No, really," she said. "I'm fine. Have a good night."

So the old man shrugged, and when he did his mouth twisted a little. Lightning cracked behind him, casting flickering, harsh shadows across his bent face. To Cassie, he was a monster. A troll. A hungry demon.

"Suit yourself," Maurice said. "Say hello to Grandma Helen for me." Then he finally retreated to his van and climbed in.

# ∽4∽

aleb leaned against a cold, black post inside the bus shelter at the corner of Fifth Avenue and Eighth Street.

He held his basketball with a limp hand against his hip and drummed on its surface with his fingertips.

He was hidden in shadows.

From where he stood, he watched the old man from the deli climb into his van. He watched the van roar to life and slowly roll off. The old man tooted the horn twice, saying goodbye to the girl he'd left behind.

Cassie waved awkwardly at the van as it drove off. Both of her arms were still wrapped around the box of food.

Caleb could almost smell it. No, he really could smell it. He could smell chicken soup. He could smell corned beef. It made his mouth water, and he smiled and licked his lips.

He stared at the slicked streets of downtown Forestville. The streetlights reflected in the puddles. They splattered and spit with the rainfall. Then they went still.

He shook and looked up. There was Cassie Cloak. Slowly, she stepped out from under the awning. The rain had stopped, and she started to walk.

Caleb stayed close to the buildings on his side of Fifth Avenue. As he walked, he started to dribble. The sound of his basketball striking the sidewalk echoed through the canyon of buildings.

He watched Cassie, too, as he walked. As he strutted along the sidewalk, he took long strides—one long stride for each of her three little steps. They reached the corner of Eleventh Street at the same time.

Caleb knew where the girl was headed. He'd heard Maurice say the name: Tall Pines, the apartment building right on the edge of the city, and on the edge of the woods beyond. It wasn't far.

# ~5~

Cassie tried so hard not to look. She knew he was there. That sound—his basketball thumping against the cement over and over, echoing through downtown. It seemed louder to Cassie than the thunder had.

But that was impossible.

It was just that in the eerie quiet right after the storm, the *boom boom boom* made her whole body quiver.

*Don't be afraid,* she told herself. *He's just a boy. He's been playing ball, and now he's walking home.*

She tried so hard not to look. But she couldn't help it. She stole a glance.

*He's tall*, she thought. *He's tall and he's watching me.*

He'd been staring right at her. When she looked—just for an instant—he was staring right at her. His big eyes shone in the dark, stormy evening like a raccoon's behind the trash cans.

And he grinned. The moment she stole a look, he grinned at her. His teeth were as big and bright as the moon on a clear night.

Then the *boom boom boom* stopped. Cassie stopped too; the light ahead said DON'T WALK.

And the boy called out to her.

"Hey," he called, and she looked again.

He was crossing. He was jogging across the street toward her. He didn't care about the puddles and the rainwater splattering up his legs, soaking his basketball shoes, soaking his socks.

She could have run. She could have at least kept walking. There was no traffic downtown at this hour on a Sunday. Why did she stop? Why did she stand there, watching him?

"You're Cassie Cloak, right?" he said as he got closer.

She didn't say anything. She might have nodded.

He reached her and stopped. He cradled his basketball under one arm and smiled down at her. He stood tall and straight. He was lean and strong. He was good-looking, too, Cassie thought. *He's also a little mean-looking*, she decided.

"I go to Perrault Middle School too," the boy said. "I'm in eighth grade."

"Oh," Cassie said. She checked the light. WALK.

"Come on," he said, and he patted her shoulder. She flinched, but she followed as he started across the street.

She knew him now, she realized, from school. She'd seen him and his big eighth-grade friends. They were rough kids. They galloped and shouted in the halls. They goofed off in front of the school before boarding their buses for home. The aides and drivers had to practically shove and drag them onto the buses most days.

Cassie would climb right on, though. She's take her seat near the middle. She'd pull out a book and open it on her lap, and then she'd stare out the window, watching the eighth-grade boys as her mind wandered.

"That sure smells good," the boy said.

Cassie didn't ask his name. She didn't know if she should. Or maybe that wasn't true.

Maybe she knew she should, but she didn't know how to do it.

"It's dinner for me and my grandma," she said instead.

"I know," Caleb said. "I heard you talking to the old guy from the deli."

"Oh," she said, but the very idea—of this boy standing near enough to hear, listening to her conversation with Maurice—sent a chill wiggling up her back and across her shoulder. She shook.

"Hey, you cold?" the boy asked.

She shook her head quickly.

"Me either," Caleb said. "I'm hungry, though. Boy, that smells good." When they reached the other corner, he started dribbling again. The ball sent a spray of water up from the sidewalk. When it bounced in a big puddle, a wave splashed up and fell onto Cassie's shoes.

"Do you mind?" she snapped.

She didn't mean to snap. She hardly meant to say anything. But that's how it came out.

The boy shot her an angry look. His smile dropped away for a moment, then came back twice as big. He grabbed his basketball with both hands, jumped ahead a couple of steps, and slammed the ball down, right into the biggest puddle on the block.

Cassie shrieked.

# ∽6∽

Caleb laughed.

He caught the basketball as it bounced back toward him, and then he bent over, slapped his thigh, and laughed.

"You should see your face!" he said. He pointed at Cassie and laughed some more.

She was drenched head to toe, and the box in her arms was splattered and stained, dark here and there from the wet.

"What's the matter with you?!" Cassie shrieked. She stomped her foot, splashing in the same puddle again.

"Whoa, watch it!" Caleb said through more laughter.

Cassie grunted and shoved past him. "Just leave me alone, you hyena!" she snapped.

Caleb chuckled one more time and stopped laughing. "Hey, don't freak out. I was just kidding around," he said. "I didn't mean to make you mad."

Cassie didn't reply. She just stomped on, farther along Fifth Avenue, as the rain started again, this time just a drizzle.

"Wait up!" Caleb called after her. He started heading in her direction.

He didn't hurry, though. He just loped along ten feet behind her, dribbling his basketball in a high, exaggerated bounce.

"Why should I wait?" Cassie snapped

without even turning around. "I don't even know you!"

"Sure you do," he said through a smile. "We go to school together."

"I'm not in a single one of your classes," she said.

"You know what I mean," Caleb said. He watched her ahead of him, her bright red slicker squeaking and swishing back and forth as she walked.

Cassie wasn't taking short strides anymore. She was stomping and hurrying along the avenue. Still, as tall as he was, he didn't have to try too hard to keep up.

"It sure is nice of you to visit your grandma," he said, trying to figure out what to say. He really hadn't meant to make her mad. "Is she sick or something?"

Cassie stomped her foot and stopped. Caleb stopped too, still behind her.

"Yes!" she said. "She is, actually!" It was the maddest she'd been so far. Obviously Caleb had asked the wrong question.

"Sorry," he said, kind of meekly. "Is it serious?"

She shrugged. Her slicker squeaked. She pulled up the big red hood. Caleb took that as a yes.

"Hey!" he said in the brightest voice he could manage. "You should get her some flowers."

She shrugged again.

"Honest," Caleb said. "The grocery on the next corner is open late. They probably have bouquets."

Cassie looked at him over her shoulder. He nodded, and she smiled.

"Good idea," she said. "Thanks."

"Sure," said Caleb. He took a long, deep breath through his nose.

The smell of chicken soup and warm sandwiches filled his soul. His stomach growled and roared.

"I better get home," he said. "Bye, Cassie."

"Bye," she said.

7

"I don't know your name," Cassie said as the boy turned and started off along Thirteenth Street.

He turned, and the light from a street lamp shone down from behind him.

"My name is Woolf," he said. "Caleb Woolf."

"Bye, Caleb Woolf," Cassie said. The rain started falling harder.

"Bye, Cassie Cloak," he said as he started off again. "See you soon."

\* \* \*

The grocery store on the corner was still open. Just inside the front door, on a tiered wooden display, were buckets of flower bouquets, all premade and wrapped in thick cellophane.

Cassie stood in front of them, letting her gaze fall from one to the next and the next. There were too many, in every color and every size, and she couldn't decide.

Her phone rang in her pocket. Quickly, she set down the heavy box of food and dug into her jeans pocket.

"Hi, Mom," she said.

"Cassie!" her mom said. Her voice was too loud, like it usually was on the phone. Cassie could tell she was anxious, too. "I just got off the phone with your grandma. We're both worried sick!"

"I'm fine," Cassie said. Maurice's troll face flashed across her mind. An instant later, she remembered Caleb Woolf's toothy grin. Her breath caught in her chest.

"Why aren't you there yet?" her mom pleaded. "You should have been there ages ago!"

"It's raining!" Cassie squealed back at her mom. "I had to wait for it to stop. Also I decided to pick up some flowers."

The phone was quiet a moment.

"Hello?" Cassie said, squinting at the phone.

"Hi," her mom said. "Okay, sweetie. We just worry about you. Now hurry along and get to your grandma's apartment so we know you're safe."

"I will," Cassie said. Her eyes settled on a

simple bouquet of small yellow flowers. "You'll pick me up at eight thirty, right?"

"Right-o," her mom said. Cassie could hear that she was smiling now. She hung up, bought the flowers, and laid them on top of her box of food. It was only another couple of blocks to Tall Pines.

~ 8 ~

Caleb stood at the far corner, hidden in shadow, and watched Cassie Cloak step into the late-night grocery store.

He counted to five to make sure she wasn't coming right back out. Then, with his basketball tucked under his arm, he sprinted back up Thirteenth Street.

At the avenue, he didn't stop. He turned hard to the right and ran as fast as he could straight to Tall Pines.

The storm had fully passed Forestville. Up ahead, low over the woods beyond the city, Caleb could see the flat bottoms of dark, heavy clouds. Thunder clapped. Lightning crashed across the sky, threatening to connect with the treetops.

At the apartment building's front door, Caleb stopped. He tossed his basketball behind the shrubs that flanked the main entrance. He didn't think anyone would want him to bring it inside, and behind the bushes it would be hidden well enough.

Caleb pushed through the front door. He tried the second door, but found it locked.

A phone hung on the wall beside the door. Next to the phone was a list of names.

Caleb ran his finger down the list. "Abramson . . . Bennet . . . Breslin . . . ah!" he said, grinning. "Here it is: Cloak. Number 516."

He grabbed the phone and dialed the number. It rang several times.

He nearly gave up. But finally a woman answered. Her voice was deep and husky, like she was very tired. Her accent, too, betrayed her age. It was just like the old man's at the deli.

"You're late," she said.

Caleb didn't speak. He held his breath, hoping the old lady wouldn't press for a response.

A moment passed. The woman sighed. "Just a second," she said, as if she were out of breath.

Caleb quickly set down the phone. A few seconds later, there came a loud and irritating buzz. The second door unlocked. He slipped in, letting the door close behind him. He hurried to the elevator and soon was on his way to the fifth floor.

The hallway smelled of lemon-scented cleanser. The lights—long and white—flickered as he passed under them. He heard televisions and laughter coming through the door as he passed Apartment 507.

He passed Apartment 511. There were kids screaming and running, thumping into walls. "Quiet down!" their mother shouted, and everything went silent.

At 516, Caleb found the door open, just a little. Cassie's grandmother must have opened it for her after buzzing the downstairs door. Caleb just strolled in. He let the door close and lock behind him.

The apartment was mostly dark. A light shone in the kitchen and down the little front hall. Caleb could smell flowers and tea.

"I've set the table," Cassie's grandma called from the other room. "And please, dear, take a moment to hang up your raincoat in the bathroom. I don't want you dripping water all over my apartment."

Caleb pulled off his hoodie and tossed it into the bathroom as he walked past. His basketball shoes squeaked and squished on the parquet floor.

"Your shoes, too!" Grandma called out. Then she muttered under her breath, "Fool child."

Caleb smiled. He stepped into the light of the kitchen, grinning as big and bright as all outdoors.

Grandma dropped her teacup. It shattered as it hit the ceramic tile floor.

# ～9～

Grandma buzzed her in without a word. She usually said "Hello," or "You're late," or "Come on up, Cassandra!"

But this night, the door buzzed an instant after Cassie called 516. The intercom phone went quiet immediately after.

"She must be really annoyed," Cassie said to herself.

The elevator bumped and shook its way

up to the fifth floor. She pulled out her phone to check the time: nearly an hour late. And as usual, no service in Grandma's building.

"Must be made of lead blocks or something," Cassie muttered. She walked down the hall on the fifth floor, looking at the bars on her phone display. She'd have one, then none, then one again.

The door to 516 stood just a little open, as always. "Knock, knock," she called into the dark apartment. "Grandma?" She pushed the door open all the way with her foot.

She could smell Grandma's jasmine tea. She could also mell a bouquet of flowers. *Oh well,* Cassie thought, thinking about the bouquet she'd picked out. *Can never have too many flowers, I guess.*

"Grandma?" she called.

She set down the box of food and pulled off her red raincoat. It wasn't so wet anymore, so she hung it up next to the door. She left her shoes on the mat and carried the box to the kitchen.

"Where are you?" she said, setting the food on the table. It was set for the two of them, and the kitchen light was on and flickering, like always. The bouquet of flowers in the center of the table was bright yellow.

She must be in the bathroom, Cassie decided, and she began unloading the big box from Maurice's. "I got extra soup," she called. Some noise came from the bathroom, but no response. "I thought it might make you feel a little better."

In the bathroom, behind the closed door, something fell and shattered.

"Grandma?" Cassie said. She stepped slowly down the dark back hall toward the bathroom. The light from inside shone under the door, sending shadows of hanging family photos in long, angular shapes up the hall walls and onto the ceiling.

A chill struck Cassie's shoulders and she shook. "Grandma?" she said. "Are you okay?"

No answer. She reached very slowly for the doorknob. "I'm coming in," she said. The moment her hand was on the knob, the door burst open, knocking her onto her back.

Her head struck the parquet floor hard— too hard. The last thing she saw was a vaguely familiar face with a big, white smile. As she drifted out of consciousness, the face became a wolf's face, baring its fangs in a wicked grin, the look of hunger about to be sated.

# ~10~

Caleb dropped to one knee beside the girl. "Oh, man," he said to himself. "I didn't mean to knock her down."

Cassie's belly moved up and down, Caleb noticed. He could even see her pulse on her throat. "She'll be okay," he said to himself.

He looked back into the open bathroom. Cassie's grandma lay on her belly on the floor with her hands and feet tied and tape placed over her mouth.

"Sorry," Caleb said. "She'll wake up in a minute, I think." Then he jumped to his feet and ran for the kitchen. The box was empty, its contents placed out on the table.

There was soup—two big containers of it. There was a small cake in a paper box. There were two foil packages—sandwiches, probably. There was a plastic box, too, filled with cubes of something—marbled with chocolate, it looked like.

Caleb grabbed the sandwiches—both still in their foil wrappers—and the plastic container of something that looked like chocolate.

Then he ran for the apartment door, made sure it was locked behind him, and took the stairs all the way down.

\* \* \*

Caleb sat on a bench beside the basketball

court. One sandwich was already gone, down his hungry gullet. He peeled the foil off the second. This one was turkey and cheese, drowning in mayo.

He smiled his toothy grin at it and licked his lips. He could still taste the mustard and corned beef from the first sandwich on the edge of his mouth.

That's when it struck him that he'd left his hoodie in Apartment 516.

# ~11~

Cassie woke up with a headache and blurry vision. She stumbled to her feet, holding the wall for support. She knocked a framed photo from the wall, and its glass shattered on the parquet floor. She hurried to the bathroom.

"Cassie," Grandma said when the girl had removed the tape on her mouth. "I thought it was you at the door. That's why I let the person in."

"I know, Grandma," Cassie said. "Who was he?" She hadn't even gotten a look at him—not that she could remember. All she could see when she tried to recall his face was the hungry face of a sinister wolf.

"I don't know," Grandma said. She shook her head and sat up, rubbing her wrists where they'd been tied. He'd used the laces from his sneakers. They were wet and tight, and they left red welts on her skin.

"Oh, Grandma," Cassie said. "Are you okay?"

Grandma nodded. "Aside from the rash on my wrists, that is," she said. Cassie helped her to stand. "And it seems he took our supper, I'm afraid."

Cassie staggered to the kitchen. "Not all of it," she said.

Grandma put a hand on her back and picked up the old phone from the kitchen wall. "Never mind," she said. "I'm not hungry anyway. But I'm going to call the doctor for that head of yours. Could be a concussion."

"Oh, Grandma," said Cassie. "I'm fine." Her vision was back to normal. "I'll just pop a couple of aspirin."

She started for the bathroom, but Grandma grabbed her wrist and put her in a chair at the kitchen table.

"Nonsense," said her grandma as she punched the buttons on her phone. "Doctor Hunter is right here in the building. He'll be happy to come up."

~12~

Caleb was so tired, and so full of soup and meat and . . . whatever that chocolate stuff was. It was nutty and smooth and rich. He wanted more of it.

But he couldn't think about that now. He had to get his hoodie back—somehow.

With any luck, the girl was still passed out on the hall floor. If she was, Grandma would still be helpless too.

He ran. He wasn't moving so fast now, though. His gut was heavy with food and his muscles ached from a long day of playing basketball, not to mention tricking Cassie and her grandma. That had taken a lot of running.

The storm was past now. The night sky was clear, and the full moon shone over Forestville. It reflected in the wet streets and the puddles at the corners.

Caleb's shoes—now without their laces— slipped up and down his heels as he jogged through downtown Forestville. He thought about abandoning them completely. He could stay on the grass the whole way to Tall Pines.

But no. His mom would kill him if he showed up tonight without his sneakers. They hadn't been cheap, after all, and he'd only convinced her to buy them for him after weeks of pleading. She'd probably make him quit the basketball team at school rather than buy him a new pair.

It was bad enough he'd need new laces. How would he explain that, anyway?

*Idiot*, he thought as he ran. *All for a couple of sandwiches. What was I thinking?*

But it was too late to change his mind now. He had to get that hoodie back. He was pretty sure Cassie hadn't seen him before she'd collapsed, and her grandma—well, she wouldn't recognize him anyway. He'd just have to make sure she never saw him again.

How hard could that be?

# ~13~

"That'll be a nasty bump," Doctor Hunter said. "Keep the ice on it for at least twenty minutes, okay?"

Cassie nodded and pressed the towel, wrapped a bag of frozen peas, against her head a little more firmly.

"Thanks for coming up," Grandma said.

The doctor shrugged. "It's no trouble," he said. Then he added, more quietly, "Keep a close eye on your granddaughter, though. These head injuries can really sneak up on a person."

"I will," Grandma assured him. She smiled at Cassie. Cassie rolled her eyes.

"Now, then," the doctor said, and he pulled his phone from his pocket. "Let's see about getting a police officer down here."

Grandma sat down and nodded gravely. "So sad," she said. "What is this neighborhood coming to?"

"Yes, is this the police station?" the doctor said into his phone as he stepped out of the kitchen.

Grandma put a hand on Cassie's knee. "How's your head, sweetie?" she said.

"It hurts," Cassie said. "A little."

"You'd better call your mom," Grandma said.

With a groan, she stood. Then, to Cassie's

surprise, she pulled three bowls from the cupboard.

"What are you doing?" Cassie said, looking up from her phone's keypad.

"No sense in letting this soup go to waste," Grandma said. "I expect Doctor Hunter will join us for a bowl, too."

Cassie managed a smile as her mom answered the phone at home.

"Hi, Mom," she said. She took a deep breath. "First of all, I'm fine."

~14~

Caleb had no breath. He squatted just outside the shrubbery that lined the Tall Pines Apartments' grounds.

Sweat ran down his face. His arms were wet. His shoes were soaking, and his feet were blistered. The night air was chilly, though, and he shivered as he caught his breath.

A police car, with its blue and red lights spinning and flashing, sat right on the sidewalk in front of Cassie's grandmother's apartment building.

"I'm too late," he muttered. He rubbed his hands together and breathed warm air onto them. "No way I can get back in there now, not with the police here."

He took a deep breath and scanned the area. No one was around.

"Tomorrow," he said to himself. Then he scurried away, into the darkness. When he was around the corner, he stood up and took off running for home.

# ~15~

The police officer had a lot of questions for Cassie and her grandma.

What did the boy look like? They couldn't say. It was so dark. All Cassie could remember was a grinning wolf.

Did he have a weapon? They didn't know. Everything happened so fast. Grandma didn't put up a fight, after all, and Cassie was knocked out by the parquet floor.

What was he wearing? Cassie shrugged. Grandma said she thought she remembered a black sweater. Maybe a sweatshirt.

The police officer had a look around the apartment. He reminded Grandma to make sure she knew who was downstairs before she buzzed anyone into the building. Finally, just as Cassie's mom arrived to pick her up, the police officer left.

"I don't feel great leaving you alone tonight, Mom," Cassie's mother said. "Come stay with us."

"Nonsense," Grandma said. "I'll be fine."

Cassie's mom gave Grandma a long look. Finally she sighed. "I know you're a stubborn lady," she said, standing up from her seat at the kitchen table. "I'll just use the restroom and Cassie and I will be out of your hair."

Grandma put a hand over Cassie's hand. "I'm sorry, dear," she said quietly.

"For what?" Cassie asked.

"For letting that maniac in here," she said. "This whole mess was my fault."

"I just wish I'd gotten here on time," Cassie said. "If I had, this never would have happened."

Mom came into the kitchen. "Is this yours, Cassie?" she said. She was holding up a black hooded sweatshirt. It was sopping wet.

"No," Cassie said. She looked at Grandma, then quickly back at the sweatshirt. "It's his, isn't it?"

"His?" Mom repeated.

Cassie's body went cold. She jumped out of her chair and grabbed the hoodie. "It's the maniac who knocked me out," she said.

She spun to face Grandma and added, "And I know who he is."

# ~16~

Cassie planned every minute of it.
It wasn't raining, but she wore her red raincoat.

She stalked the halls of Perrault Middle School with her hood up, casting a shadow over her face. Her mind raced with sinister plans of revenge and justice.

The school was mostly empty that early in the morning. She'd gotten there early, quite on purpose, so she could be ready for Caleb when he reached his locker.

At 7:30, the halls began to fill as the buses arrived in front. Cassie stood in the stairwell closest to Caleb's locker, and she watched and waited.

By 7:45, most students were already at their first class. The first bell would ring any minute.

Still, Cassie stood. Cassie watched and waited.

Finally, with only seconds until the first bell, Caleb appeared. He ran down the hall with his backpack slung over one shoulder. When he reached his locker, he hurried to open it and dropped the bag at his feet.

Cassie stepped quietly out of the shadows and stood behind the boy.

When he stood up and turned around, he jumped. "Ah!" he said. "You—you scared me. What are you doing?"

"Doing?" Cassie said, smiling. She pulled off her hood. "I'm not doing anything."

"Okay," Caleb said. He tried to shove past her, but Cassie stepped to the side to block him. "I have to get to first period," Caleb said.

"I know," Cassie said. "I just want to apologize for yesterday."

"What?" Caleb said.

"I should have offered to share that big supper my grandma and I had," Cassie said. "That was very rude of me."

"Oh," Caleb said, looking at his feet. Cassie noticed the laces were missing from his sneakers. A burst of anger flooded her chest: he'd used them to tie up Grandma.

"I want to make it up to you," Cassie said. "Will you come to my grandma's apartment for supper?"

"Really?" Caleb said. He shuffled in place a little. "Tonight?"

Cassie nodded.

"Oh, I don't know," Caleb said. "Um, I'll think about it, okay?"

Cassie smiled. "Sure," she said. "I'll get whatever you want from Maurice's, too. It's on me and my grandma!"

She made a point of looking at his feet and asked, "What happened to your sneakers?"

"Nothing," Caleb said. He slipped away and started down the hall. "I have to go," he called as he ran to his first class.

Cassie stood there, grinning, even as the first bell rang. She was late, but she didn't care. The plan would work.

## ~17~

aleb couldn't concentrate on his classes at all. All he could think about was Cassie Cloak. Her face flashed through his mind whenever he blinked. When his math teacher, Dr. Maple, asked him to come up to the board to solve for X, Caleb stumbled out of his desk.

At the front of the room, his mind reeled. The dry-erase marker in his hand felt like it weighed fifty pounds. His hands sweated. He dropped the marker twice before making a single mark on the board.

He scribbled mindlessly. He was not math genius, after all, but mostly his mind was elsewhere. As he frantically added numbers and symbols and x's and y's to the board, he thought about Cassie, in that sinister red coat of hers. He thought about his hoodie, balled up on the floor of Grandma's apartment. He remembered the taste of those sandwiches in his mouth.

He'd nearly forgotten where he was and what he was doing by the time he lowered the marker from the board. He stood back and looked at what he'd done.

The class laughed behind him. Dr. Maple cleared his throat and said, "Shush."

On the board was a series of large, wild numbers and letters. Total gibberish. At the bottom, Caleb had written "X=Cassie Cloak."

$$\frac{(a+b)-c}{a^2+b^2+b^2}$$

$$y^2 + 7x + y / 3a^2 - 2x \cdot b$$

$$3x + y/2x$$

$$x =$$

CASSIE

CLOAK

$$3^2 + 12 >$$

# ~18~

Cassie couldn't concentrate on her classes at all. It didn't matter much. She was far ahead in English class. In math, they had dozens of problems to solve independently. And as for Spanish, Cassie was fairly sure she spoke the language better than her teacher.

All she could think about was Caleb Woolf.

The night before, after her mom found that black hoodie, and after Cassie identified it—to herself—as belonging to Caleb, Cassie and Grandma agreed to turn the shirt over to the police right away.

Then, the moment Mom left the kitchen, they'd got to scheming.

"Let's not go to the police," Cassie said. She narrowed her eyes at the light fixture hanging over the kitchen table.

"No, let's not," Grandma said.

"We'll take care of this ourselves," Cassie said. She thought about Caleb's grinning face. Of course it was him! Why hadn't she realized it sooner? Who else grinned like a wolf—a hungry, conniving wolf?

"Definitely," Grandma said. "Do you have a plan?"

Cassie did. And now it was in motion.

★ ★ ★

After Spanish class, Cassie pulled up her hood and entered the crowded hallway of Perrault Middle School. No one seemed to notice her—they usually didn't.

But Cassie knew one person would recognize the red coat. She moved slowly through the halls toward the cafeteria.

Caleb was tall—taller than most of the eighth-grade boys. She saw his face, near the cafeteria doors, and he saw her. Cassie could tell.

His eyes went wide. His grin—that toothy grin he always wore—was gone.

He hurried into the cafeteria. Cassie slid through the crowd and followed him. She slipped past the back of the line. She ignored people saying, "Hey!" and "No cuts!" She stopped behind Caleb.

"Hi," she said.

He didn't look at her. Cassie thought he couldn't look at her.

"Did you decide?" she said. "About dinner." Before he could answer, she added, "Is that a new sweatshirt?"

It was a bright green one, and it looked a little big.

"What?" Caleb said, like he had just remembered where he was. "No. . . . It's—it's my brother's."

"It's too big on you," Cassie said.

"What do you want?" Caleb snapped.

*Snapped like a wolf,* Cassie thought.

She smiled at him just as pleasantly as she could.

"Fine, I'll come," Caleb said. "I'll come to dinner at your grandma's apartment."

"Great!" said Cassie. She hopped a little. She didn't even have to fake it. She was thrilled he'd be coming to dinner. Ecstatic.

Caleb moved forward in the line. Cassie followed.

"Leave me alone!" Caleb snarled.

"Don't you want to know what time?" Cassie asked. Her smile was tight and thin.

Caleb grunted.

"Seven o'clock," Cassie said.

"Fine," said Caleb under his breath.

Cassie's heart raced. She took deep breaths. It took all of her willpower not to run out of the school that very instant, right to Grandma's—clear across Forestville—to start getting ready for dinner.

# ～19～

The girl finally walked away. Caleb's heart pounded in his chest behind the borrowed green sweatshirt of his brother's. Suddenly it struck him. He left the line.

He dodged between people and trays and tables and trash cans. He spotted the red hood. He grabbed her by the arm. She spun to face him—her mouth open, her brow raging.

"Where?" he said without breath.

"What?" Cassie said.

"Where does she live?" he said. "Where does your grandma live?"

"Oh!" Cassie said. "Don't you remember?"

*Remember?* he thought. *Oh no. She knows. She really knows.*

He tried to laugh. "Like I've had dinner with your grandma before?" he said. He grinned. His biggest, toothiest grin. He forced it onto his face.

Cassie smiled. "Silly," she said. "We talked about it yesterday, remember? Tall Pine Apartments."

"Oh yeah!" Caleb said.

His heart slowed down a little. She didn't know. He was safe. "I remember now. See you later."

Cassie smiled at him. Then she turned and left the cafeteria.

# ~20~

"So much to do," Cassie said as she hurried through downtown Forestville. "So much to do and not a lot of time."

She'd ducked out of school early. No one would care. No one would even notice. Mom already knew Cassie wasn't going home after school. "I want to check on Grandma," Cassie had told her over breakfast that morning.

Mom had looked at her adoringly. "That's very sweet," she said. "I don't know if I like the idea of you being downtown on your own, though. I mean, after what happened and everything."

"I'll be back before dark," Cassie said. She kept a serious look on her face. Inside, she was grinning.

She wasn't feeling very helpless, truth be told. That morning, she'd felt like a predator herself.

\* \* \*

Downtown Forestville was crowded at three o'clock on a Monday. The streets were full of shoppers and office workers. The stores were open. The restaurants were open. It was a sunny afternoon, and some people were having a late lunch at the sidewalk cafés.

Maurice leaned on the door of his deli. He smiled as Cassie walked by.

"Hello, little Cassie," he said.

Cassie waved, but she didn't stop.

Her part of the plan was to get Caleb to Grandma's apartment at seven.

The trap was up to Grandma, and Cassie was dying to see what she'd come up with.

# ～21～

C aleb tried to take his mind off it. At the court that afternoon, he snapped at his friends and growled and grunted so much that eventually they'd given up on him.

"You're in a foul mood today, man," said Andrew, the last of his friends to leave the court. He rocketed the basketball at Caleb. Caleb caught it.

"Whatever," said Caleb. "So go home."

"I plan to," Andrew said. "Later." And he walked off.

Caleb was alone, which was how he wanted it anyway.

A lone wolf.

It was only four o'clock. Three hours till he was supposed to be at Cassie's grandma's place.

*I should just skip it*, he thought. He shouldered the ball at the top of the three-point line and took a shot.

Air ball.

He watched the ball roll on the grass toward the playground, where a few younger kids were playing while their moms looked on from nearby benches.

*I'll just skip it*, he thought again. *This is stupid. What is that weird Cassie girl going to do if I just don't show up at her grandma's house? Nothing.*

He walked slowly to collect his ball.

He found the basketball up against the big sand pit on the edge of the playground and scooped it up.

*But my hoodie*, he thought. *I have to get it back. If no one's seen it yet . . .*

He tucked the ball under one arm as he walked back to the court.

*They must have seen it,* he realized. *Then this is a trap. And if I go, I'll be walking right into it.*

*I'm not going to go. No way.*

His stomach growled.

He reached the foul line and stared up at the orange rim of the basket.

If it wasn't for the hoodie, he'd go. Just for the food.

*But she wouldn't recognize it,* he thought. *No way. It's just a black hoodie. I'm not the only one who has one. Probably everyone in the whole world has a black hoodie.*

He took a shot.

The ball slammed into the rim and bounced off. He watched it fly off the court and clear into the street. It bounced across and rolled into the gutter.

~22~

"Are you sure about this?" Cassie asked. She sat at the kitchen table while Grandma slid a huge roast into the hot oven.

"Quite sure, yes," Grandma said. She closed the oven, and then stirred the big pot of simmering chicken soup on the stove.

"We're not going to actually feed him, are we?" Cassie asked.

"Of course not," said Grandma. "But

the boy isn't stupid, even if he is a dirty little dog—a terrible person."

"Grandma!" Cassie said.

"He is," Grandma insisted. "And he'll be having second thoughts about coming here tonight." She turned from the stove and put her fists on her hips. The wooden spoon she wielded jutted out from her side like a dagger. "Really, Cassie," she said. "I wish you hadn't mentioned his sweatshirt."

Cassie shrugged. "I couldn't help it," she said. "You should have seen him. Squirming and afraid."

"I know," Grandma said. "But he must realize we found the hoodie now. He'll suspect we're setting him up."

"Maybe so," Cassie said.

"The point is," Grandma went on, "we need every possible thing to seem right. To seem normal."

"I know," Cassie said.

"We need that boy to smell this food from clear across Forestville," Grandma said as she put down the spoon and went to the window. She threw it open and waved her towel in front of the window. "Fly, scents of supper! Fly!"

Cassie giggled.

She could just imagine Caleb on the basketball court with his friends. He'd smell the roast and the soup. It would be so distracting that he'd miss a foul shot. His nose would tickle, and he'd practically float the whole way here, lured by the delicious aroma of Grandma's cooking.

# ⁓23⁓

The sun just peeked over the top of Forestville's tallest building. Caleb sat on his basketball, watching the sunset, trying to ignore the rumbling in his stomach.

He could go home and face his obnoxious older brother and doting mother. He could stay here on the basketball court until his brother came to find him, sent out by their mom, both of them angry and red-faced.

Or he could go to Tall Pines. He could pretend he's never been inside before. He could sit down with Cassie and her grandma and hope they're not up to something.

"I'll think about it," he said to himself. He stood up, cradled his ball under one arm, and started walking toward Tall Pines. "I'll think about it while I walk."

And think about it he did. He couldn't think about anything else, in fact, because clear across Forestville, he was sure he could smell his supper.

"Impossible," he muttered. He was probably smelling the deli, or the steakhouse on Park Boulevard, or even the fast-food chicken place behind the stadium. But his supper, all the way across town, coming from a little apartment on the fifth floor? "Impossible."

But it wasn't impossible. Caleb could have walked the whole way with his eyes closed. The smell grew stronger, and it carried him

along the streets and avenues of Forestville's downtown.

By the time he reached Tall Pines, it was as if he floated on a stream of fragrant air—a roast, chicken soup, an apple pie, a heaping bowl of mashed potatoes, rich gravy.

His eyes were half closed. His mouth hung open in a grin. His tongue nearly rolled from his mouth.

He reached up and poked at the numbers 5, 1, and 6.

"It's me," he said, breathless. "It's Caleb. Cassie invited me—"

The door buzzed. "Come right up," said Grandma. "Come right up, dearie." As the phone clicked off, he thought she might be laughing.

# ~24~

"Where's the sweatshirt?" Cassie said. She hurried around the little apartment, switching off this light, switching on that one, then reversing it.

"Don't worry, dear," Grandma said. She sat at the kitchen table, nibbling halvah. "I washed it and folded it and set it down on the table near the door."

"He'll see it?" Cassie said.

"He will if you stop futzing with the lights," Grandma said with a wink.

Cassie took a deep breath. "How can you be so calm?" she said. "I'm a bundle of nerves."

"I see that," said Grandma. "But I'm old hat with this stuff. Back in the old country—well, let's say we had our share of wolves."

Cassie smirked and dropped into the chair next to Grandma. She let her head fall onto the old woman's shoulder. When Grandma pulled her close in a one-armed hug, Cassie sighed.

"Then we're all set?" Cassie said.

Grandma nodded slowly. "The trap is set and ready to spring," Grandma said. "Now we'd better get ourselves in position."

"Or we'll become our own prey," Cassie said.

"And I for one am not quite ready to see your grandpa again," Grandma said.

With that, they both stood up. Grandma

closed the kitchen window, and then they left the apartment, leaving the door open, just the tiniest bit, for the company.

# ~25~

The ride up the elevator seemed to last forever.

Though he'd been enjoying and luxuriating in the sumptuous odors of supper for the whole walk across Forestville, here in the elevator, the smell was gone.

Caleb's brain fought with itself.

*I miss that smell*, he thought first.

*Get ahold of yourself,* he thought next. *This is a trap. The old lady and that sniveling little girl of hers are tricking you.*

*Nonsense,* he thought. *They're feeding you. Remember those smells? Oh, that roast. And the mashed potatoes and gravy. You can almost taste it, the meat falling off the bone. The steaming, simmering soup, full of chicken and vegetables and dumplings. So rich . . .*

*Snap out of it!* he thought. *Snap out of it!*

And the elevator dinged. The doors opened, and the elevator car filled with the scents of supper. He closed his eyes and smiled, letting the delicious smells rush over him.

His mind was clear once again. Nothing in the world would keep him out of Apartment 516 now.

Caleb nearly staggered down the hallway, past the screaming mothers and wild children, toward the slightly open door of Apartment 516.

"Cassie?" he said as he got close. He thumped the door twice with his fist. "It's me."

The door swung open as he knocked, and he went in.

"Should I close it?" he asked, though he still didn't see anyone inside, and no one had responded to his greetings from the doorway.

And it didn't matter, because when he'd stepped a few feet into the apartment, the door closed behind him.

He spun, surprised, and spotted the sweatshirt, folded and clean and sitting on a small table. He picked it up.

"Uh-oh," he said quietly to himself as he dropped the hoodie.

"Is anyone here?" he called out. He moved slowly along the dark hallway. A light shone into the hall from the kitchen, and Caleb could practically see the scents of his supper slithering along the walls and floor like snakes made of steam.

He rounded the corner and stepped into the light of the kitchen. His eyes fell first on the banquet arranged on the table.

It was everything he knew it would be: a huge roast surrounded by vegetables; a heaping bowl of mashed potatoes beside a ceramic gravy boat, sending delicious steam through the kitchen; a covered tureen, with its ladle beside it and with drippings of chicken soup running down one side; and a beautiful pie, with a crisscross pattern across its top. From the smell he could tell it was apple pie.

Caleb nearly fell upon the food, hungry like a wolf as he was, but something else caught his eye. In fact, it seemed to catch all his senses at once, and he felt himself snap awake.

He realized he was suddenly alert, aware of where he was, how far he'd walked. The kitchen had no air in it, he realized, and the windows were all closed and covered with steam. He couldn't catch his breath.

But that's not what startled him so. That's not what sent a cold shiver up his sweating back.

The oven door stood open. All the burners were on. But the stovetop and the oven gave no heat. All they gave was the hiss of gas entering the little apartment, filling it up.

Caleb, forgetting the feast, turned and ran for the door. He pulled and pounded, but it wouldn't open. He ran for the living room and struggled with the window, then with the door to the balcony. Both were sealed shut.

"Help!" he shouted, pounding on the big glass panes. But help didn't come. Caleb ran for the bedroom, hoping a window in there might work, even a crack—even the tiniest bit of fresh air might save him.

He collapsed in the hall, dropped to the parquet floor like a heap of rags, and everything went black.

# ~26~

Cassie rode in the back of the ambulance with the boy. Grandma sat in front. Cassie sat right next to Caleb, stroking his limp hand, feigning tears. Once in a while, she would sniff loudly.

"You okay?" the paramedic asked her. "He's going to be fine."

Cassie sniffed and nodded. "I hope you're right," she said. "He's my best friend."

The paramedic patted her shoulder. "It's a good thing you got there when you did," he said. "I just can't understand why he didn't open a window or get out of that apartment. He really could have died."

Cassie peeked out from under her red hood. "It's all my fault," she said. "I should have gotten there sooner. This is all my fault." She pretended to cry again.

"Now don't say that," said the paramedic. "It was an accident."

Cassie sniffed again, but she didn't respond. The ambulance sped through Forestville. The siren was on, and cars were pulling over to let them rush by.

"That's right, darling," Grandma called from the passenger seat in front. "Don't blame yourself, dear Cassie. It's really my fault. There's no one to blame but me. You know that. I forget things, now that I'm getting old. I feel terrible."

The paramedic caught Cassie's eye and smiled.

She smiled back, and the paramedic didn't notice anything sinister about it.

# ~27~

Caleb woke up under spotless white sheets in a spotless white room.

His vision was blurry, and for an instant he thought for sure he was dead—waking up in heaven.

But then there was beeping—like an old computer—quite near his head. Something tugged at his arm when he moved. Something pressed against his nose.

His vision cleared, and he saw tubes and wires running from here and there, to his arm and his face and his chest, and to machines and plastic bags hanging on his right and left on either side of the the bed.

The bed. Next to the bed, something red. A red shape. Cassie, with her hood.

Cassie smiled at him. Caleb felt her hand on his.

"Where am I?" Caleb said. His voice was cracked and dry.

"Oh, Caleb," said Cassie. Her voice sounded so strange. "I'm so glad you're okay."

His mind reeled. He remembered the feast—had he eaten? His memory was so fuzzy.

"It was all our fault!" Cassie said. She sounded like she'd been crying. She dropped her head and rolled it back and forth on his hand. "We're so sorry."

"He's going to be fine," said a woman's

voice nearby. Caleb found the doctor standing at the foot of his bed.

She smiled at him. "You'll be out of here really soon, Caleb," the doctor said. "Don't worry." On the way out, she dropped his file in a slot by the door.

Cassie leaned in closer. "I'm so glad you're okay," she said. Behind her, the blue curtain that encircled Caleb's bed ruffled and shook on its hooks.

"I don't get it," Caleb said.

He could remember more clearly now. He hadn't eaten. There'd been no one else there. The door had closed behind him. The windows were locked. The oven was on.

It was—

"A trap," he said. "You trapped me."

Cassie's mouth fell open and her eyes grew wide. "What?" she said. "Why would I trap you?"

"I found my hoodie, by the door," Caleb said. "You knew it was me."

"Why, whatever are you talking about?" Cassie said, her hand on her chest.

"Stop," Caleb said. He sat up, just the tiniest bit. The cables and tubes and wires prevented him from sitting up straight. "I know you trapped me. You were getting revenge."

"Revenge?" Cassie said. "Revenge for what, Caleb?"

She smiled, just a tiny bit, and Caleb was sure he was right.

He nodded and snarled. "Revenge because you and your crazy grandma knew it was me," he said. "You knew it was me who tied her up and knocked you down and stole your food."

Cassie jumped to her feet and looked shocked. "It was?" she said.

Caleb crossed his arms. Cassie grinned down at him, her teeth white and shining.

That smile made Caleb shiver.

The curtain flew back. There was Grandma, and a man was with her.

"That's enough, dear," Grandma said. She was smiling too. "You've had your fun."

Cassie shrugged, pulled up her red hood, and walked out. Her raincoat squeaked as she went. Grandma followed her.

The man, though, with his loose brown tie and wrinkled blue dress shirt, stayed right there. "I suppose you know who I am," the man said.

Caleb nodded. "Yes, officer," he said.

"They knew it was you, all right," the policeman said, sitting down in the empty chair. "They knew it was you the whole time."

Caleb stared at the ceiling.

"The only thing I don't get," the officer said, "is why you went back."

Caleb remembered the smells of that

supper, pulling him from the park and clear across Forestville. "Me either," he said. "Me either."

# Little Red Riding Hood

• ★ • ★ •

The fairytale known as Little Red Riding Hood is at least three hundred years old. It was first published in 1697 by Charles Perrault as *Le Petit Chaperon Rouge*, but the story's origins may have been even older. Some people think that the story might have originated in France as early as the tenth century AD.

In the original tale, a little girl walks through the woods, bringing food to her grandmother, who is ill. A wolf is in the woods too, and he has his eye on the girl.

He talks to Little Red and finds out where she's going. Then he distracts her by telling her to pick some flowers for her grandmother.

While Little Red picks flowers, the wolf goes to her grandmother's house and pretends to be Little Red in order to get inside. Then he swallows the grandmother and dresses up as her to wait for Little Red.

When Little Red arrives, she notices immediately that her grandmother looks strange, saying things like, "What big eyes you have, Grandmother!" But before she can escape, the wolf swallows her up.

In some versions of the tale, a hunter breaks into Grandmother's house, kills the wolf, and saves Little Red and Grandmother, who were swallowed whole and are still alive. In other tellings, the women were not swallowed at all and are rescued by the hunter before the wolf can attack.

# Tell your own Twicetold tale!

• ★ • ★ •

Choose one from each group, and write a story that combines all of the elements you've chosen.

A boy who wants to be king

A princess who doesn't want to get married

A young man who has never met his parents

A girl who has a pet bird

A palace

A tree fort

A city apartment

A farmhouse

---

A pigeon

A cow

A dog

A mouse

---

A daisy

An apple

A ruby ring

A pretzel

---

A tired mother

A fairy

A terrible queen

An elf

---

New York City

The French countryside

Japan

25th-Century America

# More
# Twicetold
# Tales

## about the author

Olivia Snowe lives between the falls, the forest, and the creek in Minneapolis, Minnesota.

## about the illustrator

Michelle Lamoreaux was born and raised in Utah. She studied at Southern Utah University and graduated with a BFA in illustration. She likes working with both digital and traditional media. She currently lives and works in Cedar City, Utah.